KT-152-696

3 MINUTE ANIMAL STORIES

This book belongs to
Megan

3 MINUTE ANIMAL STORIES

Written by Nicola Baxter
Illustrated by Andy Everitt-Stewart

Published by Armadillo Books
an imprint of
Bookmart Limited
Registered Number 2372865
Trading as Bookmart Limited
Blaby Road
Wigston
Leicestershire
LE18 4SE

ISBN 1-84322-165-9

1 3 5 7 9 10 8 6 4 2

Produced for Bookmart Limited by Nicola Baxter
PO Box 215
Framingham Earl
Norwich Norfolk NR14 7UR

Designer: Amanda Hawkes
Production designer: Amy Barton

Printed in Singapore

Contents

Come and Find Me!

Dennis the dinosaur was a very b-i-i-i-g dinosaur. One day, he found his friends Dimple and Dozy playing in the jungle.

"Can I play too?" he asked.

"W-e-l-l," said Dimple doubtfully. "If you like. We're playing hide-and-seek."

"Let me hide! Let me hide!" cried Dennis, jumping up and down and making everything shiver and shake.

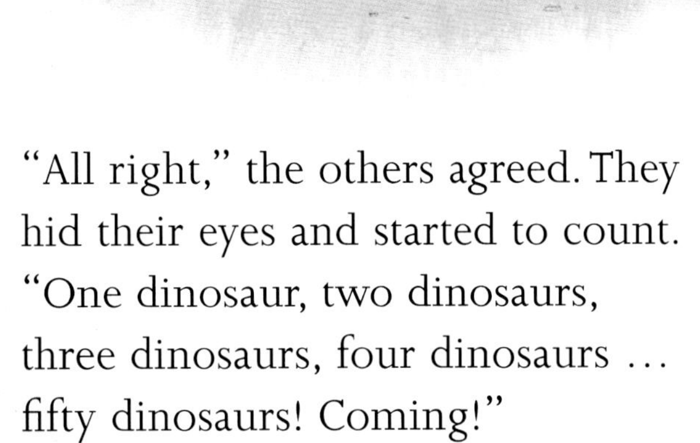

"All right," the others agreed. They hid their eyes and started to count. "One dinosaur, two dinosaurs, three dinosaurs, four dinosaurs … fifty dinosaurs! Coming!"

Oh dear! It really wasn't very hard to find a huge pink and orange dinosaur among the green leaves.

"I don't think this is going to work," said Dozy, when Dennis had been found in one second for the third time.

Even Dennis saw that this was true. Sadly, he ambled home.

That evening, Dennis didn't eat his dinner. His mother was worried. Was her dear son ill? Dennis told her everything.

Next morning, Dennis's mother took Dennis and his two friends for a picnic.

"Where are we going?" asked Dimple.

"Somewhere for fun and games," replied the largest dinosaur. "Look! We're here!"

The young dinosaurs played hide-and-seek all day long. Even Dennis.

Can you find him?

Who’s a Pretty Bird?

Most of the time, all the birds who lived at the edge of the forest were great friends. Then, one day, the peacock spread his fine tail and sighed.

“What’s the matter?” asked a passing monkey.

“Oh, nothing,” said the peacock. “I was just looking at my tail and thinking how very, very beautiful it is.”

“What? Not as beautiful as my feathers!” squawked a parrot overhead. “Just look at me! Red, yellow, blue, orange! Far brighter than you, Peacock!”

“Oooh! Rather gaudy, I think,” said a gentle voice nearby. “My pure white feathers are much more beautiful.” It was a dove, cooing in the branches, who spoke.

Well, the birds carried on arguing all that day and all that night. The other forest animals were kept awake by the noise and were not very pleased.

Next morning, as the birds still squabbled in the trees, the rest of the forest fell silent. Tiger, the fiercest animal of all, had come to see what the fuss was about.

"Well, well," he purred. "This is very useful. After all, a mighty animal like me should only feast on the most beautiful food he can find. When you have decided which of you is the most beautiful, I will be very pleased to eat the winner!"

The birds looked stunned. Then they all spoke at once.

"Some of my feathers are a little faded," said the peacock.

"My feet are not at all attractive," squawked the parrot.

"I'm really a very plain bird," mumbled the dove.

"Then you won't need to argue any more," said the tiger, as he prowled back into the forest. And they never did.

The Racing Snail

One day, a snail and a caterpillar decided to have a crawling race.

"The caterpillar is quite a bit faster," a ladybird told her friend the worm. "There's no doubt that he'll win."

"It depends how long the race is," said the worm.

"Nonsense! What difference would that make?" The worm gave a little smile and slithered away.

It turned out that the race was very long indeed – right across the garden and back again. "It will take half the summer for them to do it," said a grasshopper, "but I'll bring news back to all the other creepy-crawlies. I could travel the course in half a dozen hops."

"Ready, steady, crawl!" said a large beetle, and the race began.

Over the days that followed, the grasshopper reported on progress. The snail crept steadily on, but the caterpillar took an early lead and kept it.

Then, one day, the grasshopper jumped back with alarming news for the caterpillar supporters. "He's stopped!" he cried. "He's put on a brown coat and is hanging upside down from a leaf! I expect he needs a little rest."

But the caterpillar carried on sleeping, day after day. One morning, the snail caught up and crawled past him.

The other creepy-crawlies were all waiting on the finish line to cheer home the winner. The snail put on a final sprint, only a leaf's length from the finish. Suddenly, there was a whirring overhead, and a beautiful butterfly fluttered down. "I've won!" cried the caterpillar's unmistakable voice.

The snail took it very well. "I didn't expect to win," he said, "but it was fun trying."

"Actually," said the worm, "you *did* win. It was a crawling race, and the caterpillar-who-became-a-butterfly flew! Well done, Snail!" And all the creepy-crawlies cheered, even the butterfly.

Bartle's Revenge

There was once a cat called Bartle. He lived with the Cook family. Bartle felt the family did not look after him as he deserved. The children pulled his tail and teased him. Mrs. Cook said he was too fat and cut down his treats. Mr. Cook accused him of leaving yellow patches on the lawn (as if he would!) Granny Cook said he ate her peppermint creams.

One day, Bartle decided he had had enough. He would move in with the lady down the street who always offered him biscuits when he padded past. But first, there was something he needed to do.

He climbed right to the top of the highest tree in the garden and sat there. It took a terribly long time (and a lot of meowing from Bartle) before any of the Cooks realized where he was.

Young Tommy Cook spotted him first. "Don't worry, Bartle, I'm coming to get you," he called, and he set off up the tree.

Soon Tommy was sitting next to Bartle, but he found he couldn't get down again, with or without the cat!

When Caroline Cook spotted Tommy in the tree, she cried out in alarm, "I'll rescue you, Tommy!" and climbed up the tree herself. Soon she was sitting next to her brother, but she, too, found she couldn't get down.

The same thing happened when Matthew Cook climbed the tree, and when Mrs. Cook climbed the tree, and when Mr. Cook climbed the tree. Soon there was a branch full of five Cooks and one Bartle.

"You nincompoops!" called Granny Cook. "Don't panic! I'm coming!"

Granny Cook climbed the tree surprisingly quickly. It took her a little longer to realize that she, too, was stuck.

Bartle smiled in the smug way that only cats can … and calmly strolled down the trunk. He somehow failed to hear the shouts from above, as his mind was on a bag of peppermint creams Granny had under her pillow. It was several hours before neighbours rescued the Cooks. By then, a happy (and fatter) cat was peacefully asleep on the sofa of the lady down the street.

The Clumsy Chameleon

Carlo the chameleon was terribly clumsy. This didn't mean that he dropped things or that he kept falling from branches. There was nothing wrong with his claws at all.

No, Carlo was clumsy with his colouring. As you know, chameleons are very clever at changing how they look so that they match what they are sitting on. That way, other animals looking for a crunchy chameleon snack can't see them.

But Carlo was clumsy. He didn't concentrate. When he was sitting on a brown branch, he would suddenly start daydreaming and find that he had become yellow with stars all over his back.

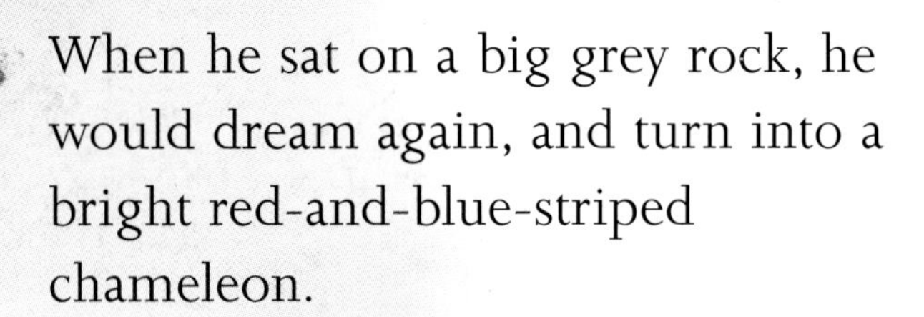

When he sat on a big grey rock, he would dream again, and turn into a bright red-and-blue-striped chameleon.

"You might just as well yell, 'Come and eat me!'" said his anxious mother. "Really, Carlo, do try to be more careful."

But Carlo simply couldn't keep his mind on the job. The inside of his head was filled with wonderful shapes and colours. Somehow, he just couldn't keep them on the inside. They had to come out.

Carlo's mother consulted Perryman the parrot. He had a reputation for being very wise.

"I know just what you should do," he said. "Get hold of the things on this list for your son. I think you'll find the problem is solved."

So Carlo's mother found smooth sheets of bark, squeezed bright dyes from fruits and seeds, and borrowed some hairs from a friendly warthog.

"Here you are, Carlo," she said, presenting him with the things she had collected, wrapped in a large leaf, "your very own painting set."

Well, no one ever saw Carlo again (though you might if you look very, very carefully), but they certainly saw his ideas and his dreams … in all the wonderful paintings that Carlo created.

Rain, Rain!

Pickle peered out. Green fields stretched far away, with hedges and gates and little lanes in between, but Pickle didn't see any of it. All he could see was the rain. For a little puppy, eager to be outside, that was a horrible sight.

Tom, the little boy who lived at the farm, thought so, too. "Let me take Pickle for a walk, Mamma," he pleaded. "Please!"

But Mamma was firm. "It's too wet, Tom," she said. "No one goes out in weather like this if they can help it."

Pickle barked. "Look!" he woofed. "Those animals are out in the rain!"

A family of thirteen ducks and ducklings was splashing its way happily down the lane.

"Well, those are ducks!" laughed Mamma. "They don't mind the wet!"

"I don't mind the wet either!" wailed Tom. "I love it!"

"Yes, but you haven't got special feathers to keep you warm and keep the wet out," said Mamma.

Pickle looked up with interest. Before anyone could stop him, he ran upstairs and into the biggest bedroom. It was a struggle to open the wardrobe doors, and dresses kept trying to tangle him up, but at last Pickle found what he was looking for. He scuttled downstairs.

"That's my best hat!" yelled Mamma.

"He was just trying to find some feathers to keep us dry," explained Tom, giving Pickle a special cuddle.

"People don't have feathers to keep them dry. They have macs and b...," began Mum, but Pickle and Tom had shot out of the room before she could finish. A minute later, *two* little figures with big, pleading eyes stood before her, holding waterproofs.

What could Mamma do? Pickle and Tom had a lovely time in the rain, dashing and splashing and chasing ... the ducks!

Around the World

When Terence the turtle decided to swim around the world, his family and friends laughed.

"Don't be ridiculous!" chortled Papa Turtle. "The world is very big. At least, I've heard it is. And you are very small. You'd never make it."

"You're not even as good a swimmer as me!" crowed his sister Teresa.

"Don't be daft, lad," said Grandad.

But Terence was determined. One sunny morning, he said goodbye to his friends and relations and swam bravely off into the ocean.

He hadn't gone very far before he began to get tired. He could still see the beach where his sister and mother were sunning themselves. Perhaps this hadn't been such a good idea after all.

Two hours later, Terence was very, very tired. His flippers trailed in the water. He was pretty sure he didn't even have the strength to swim back to the beach.

"I've been very, very silly," sighed Terence. He began to sink lower in the deep, deep water.

Suddenly, *wooooosh!* Terence felt himself flying up in the air. He somersaulted in the sunshine and fell back down … onto the back of a passing whale!

"Oh, sorry," said the whale, in a deep, musical voice. "Shall I shake you off?"

"No, no!" gasped Terence. "I was just about to sink." He told the whale the whole story.

"As it happens," said the whale carelessly, "I'm just off around the world myself. Would you like to come too?"

Terence gasped. It was a dream come true. So the little turtle and his new friend set off around the world. They had a wonderful time.

A year later, a tired but happy turtle scrambled up onto a familiar beach.

"Jumping jellyfish!" cried his father. "You did it!"

"Was it hard, darling? Was it dangerous?" asked his mother, anxiously.

Terence just smiled. "Oh no," he said. "I had a whale of a time!"

Guess Who!

"Goodness me, Willy! Stop getting under my paws!" growled Mother Wolf one morning. "Why can't you go out and play in the forest like other wolves? But remember, be back in time for lunch and don't talk to any strange humans."

Willy lolloped off into the forest. He was bored. Then, ahead, he saw something red among the trees. It was a little girl.

Now Willy knew he wasn't supposed to talk to strangers, but he didn't think there would be any harm in smiling and waving.

The little girl frowned. "I can't stop to talk to you," she said fiercely. "I'm going to my granny's house. Go away!"

Willy was frightened. Humans really were fierce! He ran off through the trees.

Panting, and feeling that he couldn't run any further, he suddenly came to a clearing with a little cottage. A very, very tasty smell was coming from it. Willy slunk forward and put his nose around the open door.

Inside, a little old lady was putting clothes away in a cupboard. Willy bounded over to do more smiling and waving, but the cottage was small, and he bounded a bit too bouncily. *Bang!* He fell against the cupboard door, which shut tight … with the little old lady inside!

Just then, a familiar voice called out. "Granny! Granny!"

Willy looked around wildly. There was nowhere to hide. Then he had an idea. He jumped into the bed and pulled the covers up to his chin.

The little girl came up to the bed. "Why, Granny," she said crossly, "you look terrible. Your eyes are red. Your ears are dirty! And *when* did you last clean your teeth?"

She peered more closely at Willy. With a shriek, he jumped out of the bed and ran from the cottage, home to the rabbit pie his dear old mother had made for lunch.

"I'll never go near a human being again," he promised her. "I was only trying to be friendly, but they're horrible!"

"Quite right, son," said his mother. And they lived happily ever after.

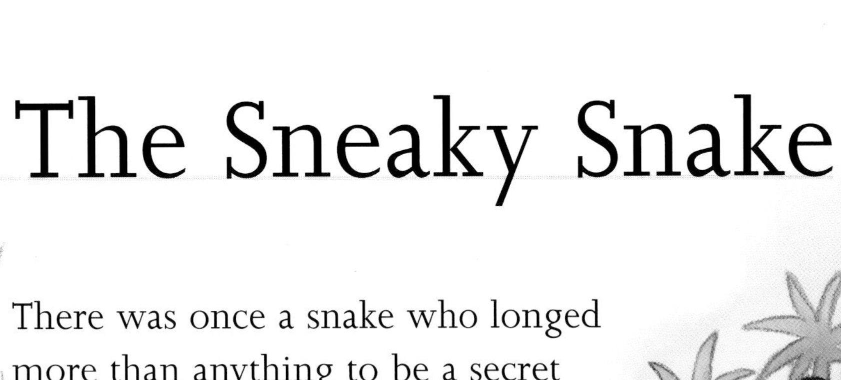

The Sneaky Snake

There was once a snake who longed more than anything to be a secret agent. The jungle animals were surprised and amused when he told them.

"You have to be good at codes," said the tree frog.

"I am," said the snake. "I've been studying. %*+^>*! See?"

The other animals didn't know what that meant, but they didn't like to say so. "All right, but you have to be good at spotting clues," said the parrot.

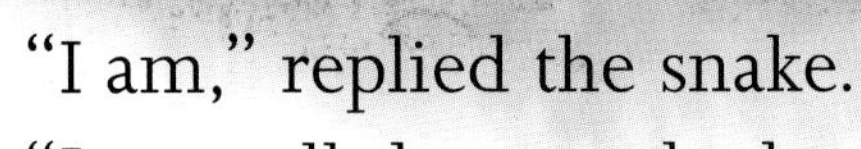

"I am," replied the snake. "I can tell that you had blueberries for breakfast."

"That's amazing!" squawked the parrot, not realizing that he had blueberry juice all round his beak.

"Hah!" said the monkey. "You also have to be a master of disguise! How can a snake look like another animal? You don't have any legs, for a start."

The snake smiled a secret smile. "I bet I'm better at disguise than you imagine," he said. "Let's test it. I'll go off into the jungle and return in disguise. You can tell each other secrets. Later, I'll tell you what they all were, to prove I was there."

The animals agreed. "He couldn't possibly dress up as a monkey," said the monkey.

"Or a frog," said the tree frog.

"I'd like to see *him* fly!" scoffed the parrot.

That afternoon, the animals gathered in the middle of a flower-filled clearing and shared their secrets. They kept their voices low and were as sure as they could be that no one could overhear them.

You can imagine how surprised they were when the snake came slithering back in the early evening. "So your middle name is Polly?" he greeted the parrot. "And you don't like water, Tree Frog? And you want to be an astronaut, Monkey?" He knew all their secrets!

The animals had to agree that the snake was a super sneaky secret agent. They never did find out how he disguised himself. Could *you* tell them?

The Singing Bird

There was once a man who was very poor. He couldn't afford a comfortable house or delicious food and drink. Every day, he got up, ate a crust of bread, and worked hard until bedtime.

But there was one thing that made him happy, and he didn't have to pay a penny for it. Outside his window, a little bird sang him awake in the morning and sang him to sleep at night. She had a beautiful song. The man felt that as long as he could hear the song of the bird, he could go on.

One day, something amazing happened. The man had a letter to say that his great uncle had died and left him a huge amount of money. The man hadn't even known that he *had* a great uncle, so the news came as a great shock.

Of course, the man's life changed overnight. He went straight out and bought himself a beautiful house in the mountains. He didn't even bother to pack up his few poor possessions, but there was one thing he couldn't leave behind. He bought a golden cage and put the singing bird in it.

"You can come and sing to me," he said, "just as you did before. You are the only thing from my old life that was beautiful, and you are beautiful still."

But when the bird in the golden cage arrived at the luxurious new house, she refused to sing. Nothing the man did would make her open her beak.

"It must be because you are in a cage," said the man. "I'm sorry. Sit on this branch outside my window and sing to me there. I know you won't fly away."

Well, the bird didn't fly away, but she didn't sing, either. She was silent and sad all day long.

Gradually, the man realized that he was sad, too. He had money, fine clothes and delicious food, but he didn't have the one thing he wanted most in the world.

"I know what you want, little bird," he whispered one day. "You want to go home, and so do I." He placed the bird gently on his shoulder and, leaving all his fine things behind, walked back to his old house.

The sun was going down as he arrived. With a sigh, the man lay down on his hard bed and closed his eyes. Outside, the beautiful voice of the bird broke into song, and the man smiled.

"I was rich all along," he said, "I just didn't know it."

The Tall Tree

Long ago and far away there was a jungle. A hot, steamy jungle. And in the middle of the jungle was a huge tree. And on this tree grew the most delicious fruit in the world. All the animals loved it. It tasted like strawberries and apples and bananas and oranges all mixed up together.

One day, a little monkey, sitting on a branch and munching one of the yummy fruits, noticed something important. There was only one fruit left. It was right at the top of the tree. He hurried to tell the other animals.

"Goodness me," said the monkey's mother. "Your father and I had better eat that fruit. Just to stop it falling into the wrong hands, you know."

"Actually, it should be mine," said a mouse. "I have ten little babies to feed. Our need is greater than yours."

"Well," said the tiger, "I am the fiercest animal in the jungle, so I will obviously be the one to eat the last fruit. Just you try and stop me!"

Suddenly the parrot laughed out loud.

"And how are any of you going to reach the fruit?" she asked. "Can you climb so high, Tiger? No? Or you, Mouse? No? And what about you, Mother Monkey? I know you can climb high, but can you climb as high as that?"

The monkey was forced to confess that she could not.

"Only a bird can reach that fruit," squawked the parrot. "And I am going to do it right now!"

The parrot flew up, up, up to the gleaming fruit. She pecked with her sharp beak … and suddenly gave a squawk. The fruit was so big and heavy that it slipped through her claws. The animals watched, open-mouthed, as the fruit fell down, down, down and hit the ground with a *thud!* It smashed into such tiny pieces that there was not the smallest crumb for anyone to eat.

"It's a disaster!" cried the monkey. But she was wrong. When the fruit hit the ground, hundreds of tiny seeds flew out into the jungle. In the steamy heat, they soon grew … and a whole forest of fruit trees kept all the animals happy!

A House for Mouse

Mouse lived in a snug little house he had built himself. It nestled between the roots of a hawthorn tree. He was happy there.

One day, when Mouse was out gathering berries, the farmer decided to cut the long grass at the edge of the field, and Mouse's house disappeared.

Mouse was very upset. It was late in the year. Bad weather was coming. How would he manage in the winter without a house? Mouse packed some seeds and berries into a little basket and set off to find somewhere new to live.

A mouse is very small. He doesn't need a huge house. Mouse thought it would be easy to find a snug little place. He was wrong.

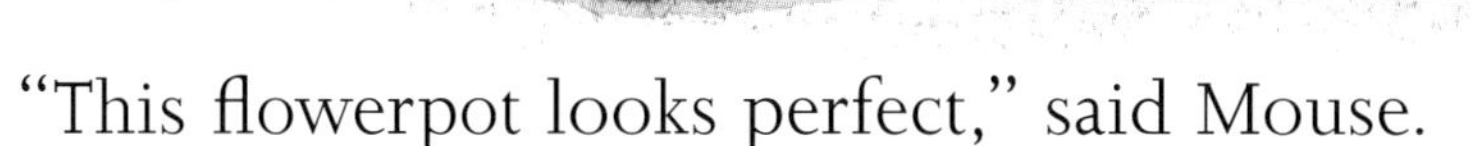

"This flowerpot looks perfect," said Mouse.

"It is perfect for me!" croaked a big brown toad.

"I could be cosy in the hole in this tree," squeaked Mouse.

"Not with me inside!" hooted a fierce-looking owl.

"I would be quite comfortable under this old shed," cried Mouse.

"Really?" asked a very large rat.

Poor Mouse tramped on for days. He soon ate his seeds and berries. He felt tired and hungry. Each night, the wind blew colder.

Then, one clear day, Mouse was scuttling along when he almost fell into the most beautiful little mouse's house he had ever seen. It reminded him of his own dear home, now gone for ever.

"This is just right for a mouse," said Mouse, "but it is so well cared for, someone must already live here."

"Yes," said a voice, "I do. But it is very lonely all by myself."

Mouse looked up into the bright little eyes of a smiling mouse who looked just like him – except that she was a lady mouse.

So that is how Mouse found a home and a wife all in one day. Years later, when his grandchildren had little bumps and bruises, he would say, "You know, losing my home was the best thing that ever happened to me. You just never know when something bad is going to turn into something very, very good."

Shhhh!

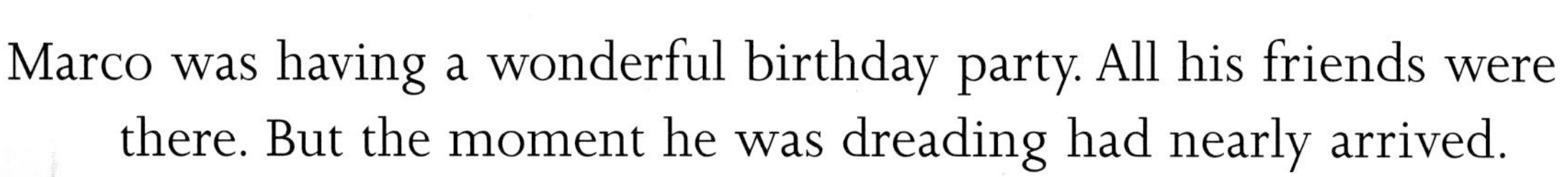

Marco was having a wonderful birthday party. All his friends were there. But the moment he was dreading had nearly arrived. In came Marco's mother, proudly carrying a huge banana-frosted birthday cake. (Marco loved bananas.)

Marco looked up at his mother as she put the cake on the table. "Please don't sing, Mamma," he whispered. "P-l-e-a-s-e!"

It was too late. She had already started on "Happy Birthday," only it was more like

"Happy Birthday!"

You see, Marco's mother had a really, really loud voice. Whenever she sang, Marco was sooooo embarrassed.

A few days later, Marco and his mother went on a camping trip with four of his best friends. Before they went, Marco made his mother promise that no matter how many campfire songs they sang, or how many Tarzan yells they called, she would never, ever join in.

The camping trip was fun, and Marco's mother kept her word, though she sometimes had to put her paws over her mouth.

On the last day, the friends (and Marco's mother) hiked through the woods to a deserted canyon. It was a fantastic day … until they reached the canyon. Just as they all safely got to the bottom, rocks began tumbling down above them. Marco's mother hurried the little ones to safety, but the damage was done. The only path up the steep sides was blocked. There was no way out.

"Help!" shouted Marco and his friends. "Help! Help! Help!" Their voices sounded tiny. No one came. Marco looked at his mother. She nodded.

"Help!" she thundered. "HELP!"

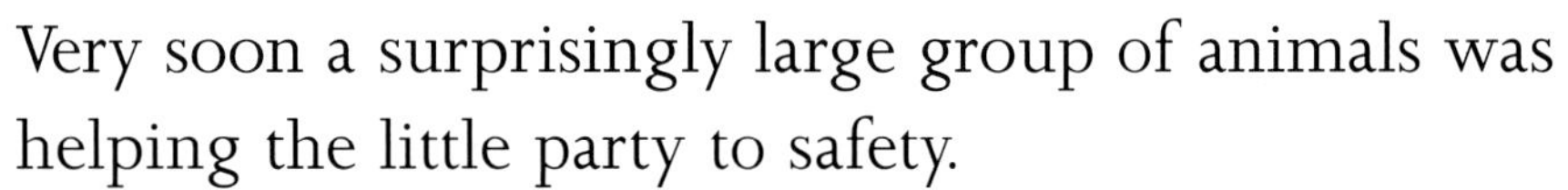

Very soon a surprisingly large group of animals was helping the little party to safety.

"I suppose it's quite useful, sometimes, having a loud voice," sighed Marco, as they tramped home.

"Can be," grunted Mamma.

"Doesn't mean you have to use it every day," said Marco casually.

"Say no more, Marco," grinned Mamma. "Emergencies only from now on!"

Mr. Noah's Problem

When Mr. Noah built the ark, he thought carefully about where all the animals would sleep. He made big stalls for the elephants and the hippos. He put a window in the roof of the giraffes' stall, so that they didn't get cricks in their necks. He made homes in little boxes for the mice and the hamsters, so that the bigger animals wouldn't stand on them by mistake.

"I really think I've thought of everything," Mr. Noah told his wife, as he watched dark storm clouds gather overhead. Mrs. Noah wasn't so sure. "What about the woodworms?" she asked.

"All taken care of," said Mr. Noah happily. "There will be plenty of room for them in the box I have made for the earwigs and the fleas."

"And what is the box made of?" asked Mrs. Noah quietly.

"Well, wood, of course!" cried Mr. Noah. Then he frowned and said, "Oh!"

"Exactly," said Mrs. Noah. She had realized that the ark, and everything in it, was made of wood. And woodworms eat wood. They make lots of little holes as they munch their way through planks and beams. And sooner or later, lots of little holes might let in water.

Mr. Noah thought hard. Then he went into his workshop and made lots of little wooden balls. "Now I must talk to the woodworms," he said.

The next day, the rain came down. It rained for forty days and forty nights. Everyone was overjoyed when it stopped at last, and the ark came to rest on the top of a mountain.

"Well done, Mr. Noah!" said his wife, giving him a hug.

"No, without you, it could have been a disaster," said Mr. Noah. "My friends and I have a present for you to say thank you." He gave a delighted Mrs. Noah a beautiful necklace of wooden beads. Each one had a tiny, perfect hole munched all the way through it for the string. I wonder how that happened...?

The Outsider

Ferdinand was a small fish. He lived near a coral reef, where the water was warm and blue. All around him swam bright little fish of every kind you can imagine. There were orange ones with yellow stripes. There were green ones with blue spots. There were red fish and purple fish and yellow fish.

But Ferdinand wasn't patterned. He didn't have long, flowing fins. He couldn't jump out of the water like the flying fish. There was nothing very interesting about him at all. He was a sludgy brown colour, and most of the time, no one noticed him.

"Everyone can't be flashy," said his mother. "You're fine as you are, Ferdy."

Ferdinand wasn't so sure. He wanted to be noticed. He tried to improve the way he looked by draping bits of seaweed around himself. It wasn't a great success. In fact, it made it even harder to spot him.

Sometimes, the other fish made fun of Ferdinand. "Oops, sorry, Ferdy," they would say, as they bumped into him. "We didn't see you there. We thought you were a patch of mud! Ha ha!"

Then, one day, as Ferdinand was lurking near a sludgy brown rock, there was a great splashing and thrashing in the water nearby. Ferdy saw some gleaming white teeth and a bright, beady eye. Luckily, the bright, beady eye didn't see him. It did see the orange fish with yellow stripes. It did see the green fish with blue spots. It saw the red fish and the purple fish and the yellow fish, too.

And it ate them all up in a single shark-sized gulp.

When the shark had eaten everyone in sight, she swam slowly off in search of another snack. Ferdy floated gently out of his hiding place and looked around. He decided that if he had to choose between being a sludgy brown fish outside a shark or a bright, flashy fish inside a shark, he knew exactly what he thought was best. And he swam home to tell his mother.

A Roaring Success

Len and Laura Lion were very proud parents. They called their first cub Leo and showed him off to all their friends.

"He's going to take after his old dad," said Len, puffing out his chest. "He'll be the raciest runner and the most powerful pouncer in the pride. And he'll probably have my magnificent mane, too."

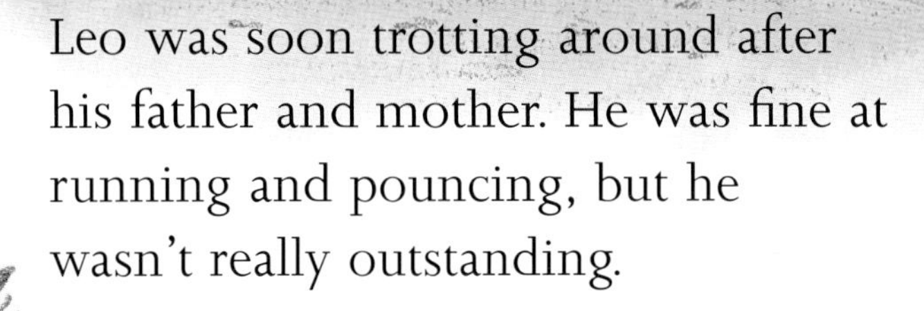

Leo was soon trotting around after his father and mother. He was fine at running and pouncing, but he wasn't really outstanding.

"Are you trying, son?" asked Len, when Leo trailed in last after a practice run. "The other cubs were miles ahead. What's the trouble? Thorn in the paw? Sniffles in the nose? You can tell me."

"I'm fine, Dad," said Leo. And he was. He just wasn't the racing, pouncing champion Len had hoped for.

"Leave the boy alone," said Laura. "He's a great cub. And his mane is starting to grow. Who knows?"

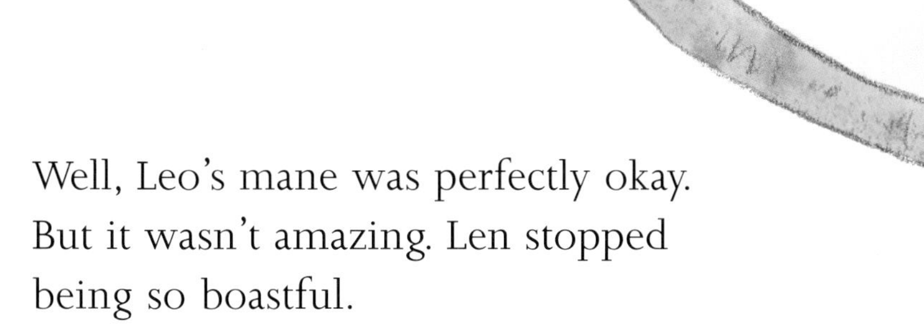

Well, Leo's mane was perfectly okay. But it wasn't amazing. Len stopped being so boastful.

Then, one day, when the older lions were out hunting, a pack of hyenas came sniffing around the clump of grass where the baby cubs and bigger young lions like Leo were resting.

At once, the nearly-grown-up lions sprang to their feet, pouncing and snarling. The hyenas took no notice. They had spotted a plump little cub in the grass. Closer and closer they came, until some of the young lions let out roars to frighten them away. They had never had to use their roars before. It did no good. Then, suddenly...

ROOoaAAaaaRRrrr!

It was Leo! The whole savannah shook at the sound. The hyenas ran off, and the grown-up lions came running back as they heard the noise.

Everyone agreed. A roar like that had never been heard before. Leo was a star at last. And Len? He is a very happy lion indeed.

Bess's Busy Day

One fine morning, Farmer Phil set off to plough the North Field.

"I won't need you today, Bess," he called to his sheepdog. "You can keep an eye on the barnyard for me."

Bess looked a little lost. She felt that her proper place was just behind Farmer Phil's left boot, or rounding up the sheep out on the hills. Then, with a small sigh, she settled down in the sun for a snooze.

But sheepdogs are busy dogs. They like to be active. When, a couple of minutes later, Doris Duck waddled past with her brood of five ducklings, Bess couldn't resist it. She jumped to her feet and began to round up those ducklings into what she thought was a more orderly line.

Doris was not pleased. "Leave my ducklings alone!" she quacked. "You're frightening them! They can walk perfectly well by themselves, thank you!"

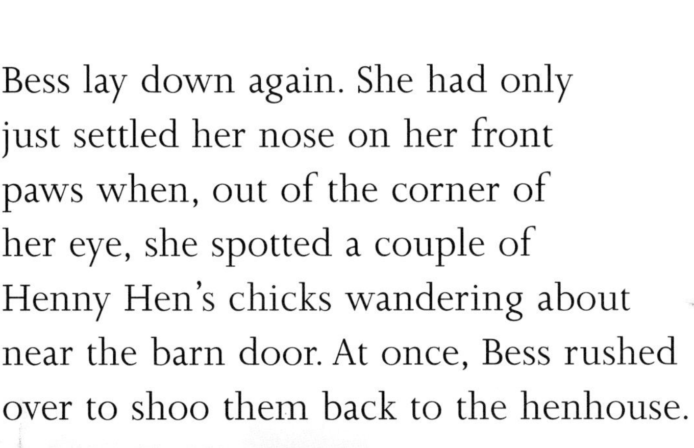

Bess lay down again. She had only just settled her nose on her front paws when, out of the corner of her eye, she spotted a couple of Henny Hen's chicks wandering about near the barn door. At once, Bess rushed over to shoo them back to the henhouse.

"Do you mind?" squawked Henny. "I'm trying to teach my chicks where everything is in the barnyard. If I wanted them to be in the henhouse, I'd shoo them there myself!"

Poor Bess! She tried to keep the piglets out of the mud, but Pedro Pig got cross. She chased the mice around the barn, until Pom the cat told her that was *his* job.

When farmer Phil came back from the fields, the farmyard was in uproar. All the animals were squawking and clucking and quacking and squeaking and squealing at once.

Farmer Phil couldn't understand it, until he saw Bess sitting with her head between her paws and looking sorry for herself.

"Don't worry, old girl," he said.
"I should have remembered.
You're not a guard dog,
you're a *working* dog. Next time,
you come with me, where you belong."

And the whole farmyard cheered!

Ten Little Frogs

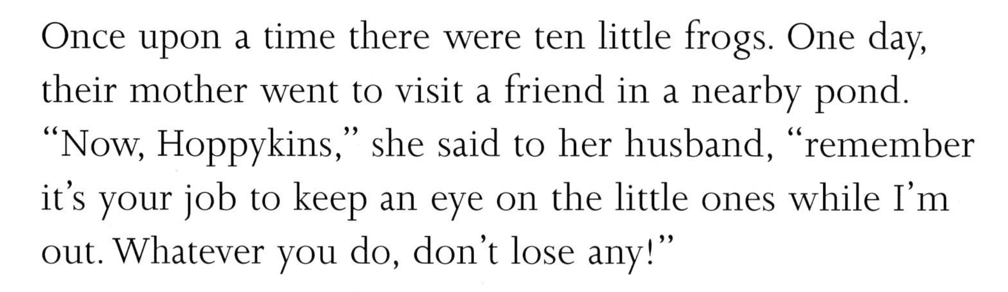

Once upon a time there were ten little frogs. One day, their mother went to visit a friend in a nearby pond. “Now, Hoppykins,” she said to her husband, “remember it’s your job to keep an eye on the little ones while I’m out. Whatever you do, don’t lose any!”

“Yes, dear,” said Hoppy. But those froglets were lively. They jumped about all over the place. Before long, Hoppy was hot and bothered.

“One, two, three, four … oh no, I’ve counted you twice,” he began. “One, two, three, four, five, six, eight, nine, ten. Hang on, I’ve got one left!”

Hoppy did his best to make the little frogs behave. He lined them all up on a log and began to count. “One, two, three, four, five, six, seven, eight, nine, ten, eleven, twelve, thirteen … what?”

Hoppy didn’t notice that the frog at the beginning kept jumping to the end, ready to be counted all over again.

Hoppy told the frogs to jump into the pond to cool down. Actually, it was Hoppy who needed to cool down. But in the water, it was even harder to keep track of them.

All too soon, the sound that Hoppy had been dreading boomed through the water. “Hoppykins! I’M HOME!”

Poor old Hoppy looked glum. He knew he was in for a telling-off. But the froglets knew their mother, too. And they guessed that if their dad got a piece of her mind, they would, too. So one by one, they came creeping out. Can you spot them before their mother does?

Quarrrk!

It was midnight in the jungle. All the animals were asleep. Monkey was snug in his nest of leaves. Parrot was perched on his sleeping branch. Snake was curled round the trunk of a tree. Lizard snored nearby. And far below, Tiger and his cubs slept peacefully on the forest floor.

Suddenly, "Quarrrk! Quarrrk!"

Everyone jumped up at the awful sound. Tiger growled and stood in front of his cubs. Lizard scampered out of sight. Snake hissed warningly. Parrot flew up, scattering feathers, and Monkey chattered with fright.

"W-w-w-w-what was that?"

Everything was quiet. The animals listened. They couldn't hear anything other than the usual rustling jungle sounds. One by one, they drifted off to sleep again. Until…

"Quarrrk! Quarrrk!"

This time, Tiger was angry. "Who's making that noise?"

But still, nothing stirred in the jungle. Once again, the animals settled down.

When the horrible noise happened for the third time, Tiger decided to act. "One of us must stay awake," he snarled, "to see who is disturbing our sleep. If this is some kind of joke, Monkey, it's not a very good one."

"It's n-n-not me!" chattered Monkey. "I'll stay awake and listen. You'll see."

So the other animals went back to sleep, and Monkey rubbed his eyes to keep awake.

"Quarrrk!" *Thud!*

Monkey fell off his branch and landed on Tiger!

"It was right in my ear!" gasped Monkey.

"Which ear?" asked Tiger.

"This ear!" screeched Monkey. "It was scary."

Tiger stared up at the branches above. "The squawking animal nearest your right ear, Monkey, was Parrot," he growled.

"I didn't do it!" squawked Parrot.

"I'm afraid you did, old friend," said Tiger kindly. "You've been sleeptalking! And I've got the answer." He tied a vine around Parrot's beak in a neat bow.

"I'll take it off in the morning," he said. "Sweet dreams, everyone!"

And that's exactly what they had.

No Place Like Home

Pauly was a polar bear. He lived with his mother in an ice cave near the North Pole. Even if he walked all day, all he could ever see was ice and the cold sea of the Arctic Ocean.

As he grew older, Pauly began to think that perhaps there might be more to life than ice and sea. He chatted to the gulls who flew overhead and heard tell of lands that were green, not white, and seas that were warm and full of bright little fish. More and more, Pauly longed to see them.

One day, a new seabird flew in to land near Pauly's cave. He didn't look like the other gulls and, when Pauly told him of his dreams, he said an extraordinary thing. "Well, that's no problem," he chirped. "I can do magic, you see."

In a flash, Pauly found himself sitting next to the bird in a completely different place! There was sand under his paws, and palm trees ran along the shore of the bluest sea he had ever seen.

"What do you think?" asked the bird.

"It's beautiful," said Pauly. "But the brightness hurts my eyes. And, oh dear, it is *so* hot!"

"No problem!" said the bird. In a flash, Pauly found himself in a cooler place. Everywhere he looked there was green grass, and lots of fences, between which animals strolled and munched the grass.

"It's a farm," said the bird. "Is this better?"

"Those poor animals!" cried Pauly. "They can't go wherever they like! And, oh dear, it is still *so* hot!"

Before he had finished speaking, Pauly found himself in yet another place. Tall, tall trees towered overhead, while a little stream sparkled by his feet. The air in the forest smelt damp and cool.

"I'm sorry," whispered Pauly, "but I still don't like it. What if those trees fell on me? And, oh dear, even here it is *so* hot!"

In the blink of an eye, Pauly found himself back in his old home. He sniffed the cold air and dug his paws into the icy snow.

"I hope you're happy!" chirped the bird. "I can't believe you prefer this to the wonders of the world I have shown you."

"But I do," smiled Pauly. As he fell asleep, the rainbow colours of the Northern Lights shimmered overhead. "Home is always the most wonderful place in the world," whispered one happy little bear.

The Tiny Friend

Long ago, a huge, hairy mammoth stomped through a forest in search of food. Although he looked scary, he was really very gentle and kind. He ate leaves and grass, but he needed a lot of both. That was why he was always on the move, trying to fill his rumbling tummy.

One day, as the mammoth was munching a bush of leaves and berries, he heard a very tiny sound and felt a tickling in his ear. He shook his head impatiently from side to side, but the sound and the tickling went on. When he kept still, the mammoth could hear that the sound was a very tiny voice.

"Please," said the voice, "oh, please, Mammoth, don't put your great foot down. My little ones are just underneath."

The mammoth looked down. He had been resting one foot on a small rock, and there, just where he was about to put his foot, lots of tiny spiders were running about.

"Please don't hurt them," begged the mother spider, who was hanging from a thread near the mammoth's mighty ear.

The mammoth was, as I said, kind. So he carefully plodded away, being careful not to put his great feet on any tiny creatures.

A few days later, as he was wandering through the forest, the mammoth heard something that frightened him very much. It was a shout. The mammoth knew that human beings liked to hunt mammoths with their sharp spears. As quickly as he could, he trotted away, the ground shaking at every step.

But the human hunters were faster. Before long, the mammoth felt spears whistling past his ears. And the shouts grew louder and fiercer. He ran forward, and squeezed through the opening of a large cave. At first it seemed a good hiding place, but as the hunters grew nearer, the mammoth realized that he was trapped. There was no other way out of the cave. He would be found for sure.

"Don't worry," said a voice that he could hardly hear above the sound of his thumping heart. "You did me a kindness. Now I will help you."

At an amazing speed, the spider spun a web across the entrance to the cave. When the hunters arrived, they shook their heads. "He can't be in here," they grunted. "This cobweb hasn't been disturbed."

Slowly, their shouts disappeared into the distance. "Thank you," breathed the mammoth, but his little friend had gone, and the huge animal never heard his tiny voice again.

Hide-and-seek

Once upon a time there were ten little bugs:

Una, Tula, Trina, Forster, Quentin,

Cicely, Septimus, Otto, Nina and Declan.

They lived with their mother in a beautiful garden.

One day, the mother bug said to her little ones, "Sweethearts, I must fly off and see how the roses at the other end of the garden are doing. You ten stay right here under this leaf. I won't be long."

The little bugs hadn't been sitting still for long before it started to rain. Water dripped from their leaf and fell … splosh! … on the ground. When it stopped at last, the sun came out. The whole garden glittered with jewel-like raindrops.

"It looks lovely," gasped Una. "Let's go and explore." Without thinking for a minute about what their mother had said, the naughty little bugs set off.

Some liked yellow flowers best and jumped onto their sunshiny petals. Others headed for blue flowers, sparkling and nodding. Otto spotted some bright red dahlias and could hardly be seen, as she was red, too! Two little bugs had fun sliding down the day-lily leaves.

When their mother came back a few minutes later, she was horrified to find her babies gone. She guessed what had happened but she knew that she had to find her little ones quickly, before a hungry bird spotted them! "It will take me ages to find them all among the flowers," she sighed. "I hardly know where to start." Do you think you could help her?

The last little bug of all was the hardest to find. At last the adventurer was found under an upturned flowerpot. Can you work out which one that was?

The Secret Pet

One afternoon, when Benjamin was walking home from school, he saw a scruffy little puppy sitting on the pavement. As he passed, the puppy put its head on one side and looked up appealingly.

"Sorry, mate," said Benjamin. "My mother won't even let me *think* about having a pet. And my dad's worse."

The puppy gave a little whine, as if to show that it understood.

Benjamin walked on, but when he paused to cross the road opposite his house, he noticed that a scruffy little puppy was sitting just behind him.

"No, no," said Benjamin, squatting down to talk to the puppy. "I meant it. You really can't come home with me. My parents would never let me keep you. They'd probably take you to the Dogs' Home."

The puppy looked at the pavement. Reluctantly, Benjamin picked up his book bag and carefully crossed the road, deliberately not looking behind him.

Over supper, Benjamin was very quiet. He couldn't help thinking about the puppy.

"Are you all right, Ben?" asked his dad. "You've hardly touched your pizza."

Benjamin didn't think it would be a good idea to mention the puppy, so he just said he wasn't very hungry.

Later, when he got ready for bed, Benjamin went to the window and pulled the curtains. Outside on the pavement, sitting in the pool of light from a streetlamp, sat a familiar figure.

All night long, Benjamin tossed and turned. It was no good. At half past three, when the house was quiet, he crept downside and carried the little dog inside.

"Just for tonight," he whispered, "and don't make a sound."

The puppy was as good as gold. He settled down on the rug beside Benjamin's bed and went to sleep.

An hour later, the whole house was woken by a terrible noise. Downstairs, what sounded like a very big dog was barking at the top of his voice. The whole family rushed downstairs to find a small, scruffy puppy pinning a shifty looking character to the sofa.

It was breakfast time before the police had carted away the burglar, and the puppy had been explained.

"Now, Ben," said his dad, "you know we've always said no pets. Your mother and I are just not keen on the idea."

Ben looked sad.

"Of course," said Dad, "guard dogs are a different matter entirely!"

Oswald Learns a Lesson

Oswald Ostrich was a very clever little bird. When I say that he was little, I mean that his mother and father towered over him, but compared with most birds of his age, Oswald was HUGE!

Oswald lived on a dusty plain. There were one or two bare-looking trees but nothing else at all for miles and miles. The animals that lived on the plain were always on the move, usually in groups with their friends and families.

Oswald was always eager for new ideas and information to fill his clever little head, so he made friends with all the animals he met. By talking to the other animals, Oswald learnt a great many things. The gazelles showed him how to play jumping games. The lions showed him how to creep up on gazelles (just to surprise them, of course). Oswald was keen to try everything.

Then, one day, Oswald met a vulture. He was an ugly bird, and Oswald was a little frightened of him at first, but it turned out that Vic, as he was called, knew a great many interesting things. Oswald never tired of hearing about all the amazing adventures Vic had had as he flew across Africa.

"Tell me more about flying," said Oswald. "Could anyone do it?"

"No, no," laughed Vic hoarsely. "Gazelles can't do it. Lions can't do it. You have to be a bird to do it."

Oswald flapped his own stubby wings. Nothing happened. He tried running very fast and flapping his wings. Still nothing happened. He tried running even faster, until even the startled gazelles were left behind, but his funny little feet never left the ground.

His dad found him sad and exhausted, flopped against a tree.

"There's something wrong with me," said Oswald. "I'm a bird but I can't fly. I'm so sorry, Dad."

Dad grinned. "Have you ever seen me fly, Oswald?" he asked. "No? Well that's because ostriches are very, very special birds. We never fly. In fact, we're very strict about it. Let chattering parrots and smelly vultures fly. We don't need to."

"Why not?" asked Oswald.

"Because we can run!" cried his Dad."We can run faster than any bird in the world! Why would we want to fly? Come on, you're a big boy now, I'll race you back."

And after all his take-off practice, Oswald was so fast he even beat his dad. He decided that he had a lot to be proud about after all.

The Cat and the Dog

Once there was a cat called Cuddles and a dog called Major. They both lived with Arianna Detrop, the famous opera singer, but they were not friends. Cuddles thought that Major was big and rough with no manners. Major thought that Cuddles was a foolish, fluffy animal who lolled about on silk cushions all day, (which, in truth, he did.)

Arianna Detrop was away a great deal. The animals hardly saw her. They spent most of their time apart or sitting with their backs to each other in front of the fire.

One day, a dreadful thing happened. During one of her most powerful performances, in the middle of a "*Tra-la-la-LA!*", Madame Detrop fell off the stage! She broke her leg and had to come home to rest.

Things changed overnight for Cuddles and Major …
and not for the better. For Major, the problem was the
singing. Madame Detrop was so keen to keep her voice
in trim while she was at home that she sang every
moment of the day. It was loud singing. Very loud singing.
Poor Major put his paws over his ears and whined softly.
He had never been so miserable.

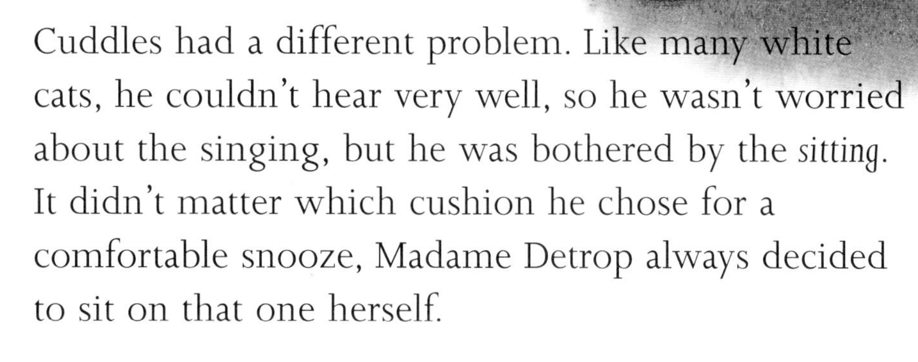

Cuddles had a different problem. Like many white
cats, he couldn't hear very well, so he wasn't worried
about the singing, but he was bothered by the *sitting*.
It didn't matter which cushion he chose for a
comfortable snooze, Madame Detrop always decided
to sit on that one herself.

Stuck at home with no exercise, Madame had been
tucking into chocolates sent by admirers. Her bottom
was not small. On several occasions, Cuddles was
almost squashed flat.

One evening, when Madame was tirra-lirra-ing from the sofa,
Major and Cuddles met on the stairs. For the first time,
they did not view each other as enemies.

"I have an idea that might solve both our problems,"
woofed Major hesitantly. "But you might
not like it." He whispered in Cuddles's ear.

"It's purrrrfect!" smiled Cuddles.

So Major found some fantastic earmuffs,
and Cuddles found a comfortable place
to snooze. They were friends at last.

The Lost Quack

It was a beautiful rainy day at the pond. *Splish! Splash! Splosh!* went the raindrops in the water. *Quack! Quack! Quack!* said the ducks. *Croak! Croak! Croak!* called the frogs. They all loved the rain.

"Isn't it lovely, darlings?" a mother duck on the bank quacked to her five little ducklings, who hadn't seen rain before.

"*Quack!*" agreed the first duckling.

"*Quack!*" agreed the second.

"*Quack! Quack!*"cried the next two.

"*Croak!*" said the fifth, and was so surprised that he fell into the water in a flurry of feathers.

Mother Duck watched anxiously as he bobbed to the surface and clambered back onto the bank.

"Are you all right?" she quacked.

"*Croak!*" said the little duckling. "When I open my beak, that's the noise that comes out. Yesterday it was a quack and today it's a croak."

"I don't like this at all," said his mother. "We'll ask Queen Swan."

The beautiful white bird was thought to be very wise. She listened carefully to what the mother duck said.

"It sounds to me," said Queen Swan, "as if someone has stolen your quack and given you a croak instead. All you need to do is to find out who is now quacking when they should be croaking."

"You mean it's one of those frisky frogs?" quacked Mother Duck. "I should have known. Leave it to me, Your Majesty. I'll soon have this sorted out."

Mother Duck knew that if she asked the frogs to croak one by one, they would be awkward and hide in the weeds. She thought of a plan.

"This afternoon," she said, "we are having a singing competition. Please line up if you want to take part. Frogs first!"

All the frogs, who were proud of their singing voices, lined up on the bank.

"Now, first I want to hear how loudly you can sing," said the mother duck. "One croak each, please, in turn. One, two, three…!"

Croak, croak, croak, croak … the frogs began … *croak, croak, croak, CROAK, CROAK, CROAK, QUACK!*

"Aha!" Mother Duck scooped the offending frog up under her wing and dragged him off to find her duckling.

"You just give him his quack back right away," she said firmly.

"It was just a joke," said the frog. "A croak joke." But he did what she asked. The little duckling was happy to be quacking once more. And even the naughty frog was pleased, because after all that, he won the singing competition!

The Egg Hunt

Oona the hen laid a beautiful brown egg every single day. She was proud of her eggs and looked forward to sitting comfortably on them for a few weeks until they hatched out into dear little fluffy chickens.

But Oona had a problem. Each day, as soon as she had laid one perfect, brown egg, the farmer came along and took it away. You see, he loved Oona's eggs for his breakfast. There never were any eggs left for Oona to sit on.

Oona was not a clever hen, but at last it dawned on her that she must do something. The answer, she knew, was to hide her eggs.

The next day, she didn't lay her egg in the henhouse. She laid it under the hedge in a nice quiet spot.

It took the farmer ten minutes to find the egg he was sure must be somewhere about.

The next day, Oona laid in the barn, high up on a bale of straw. Even so, the farmer found the egg after hunting for fifteen minutes.

And so it went on. Each day, Oona laid an egg. And each day, the farmer hunted and hunted until he found it. This happened for weeks and weeks. One day, it took the farmer all morning to find the egg, and he wasn't very pleased to have to wait so long for his breakfast!

Poor Oona was running out of places to hide her eggs. Then Willow the cat, who was very clever, whispered in her ear.

"Are you sure?" clucked Oona.

"Pretty sure," purred Willow.

The next day the farmer could not find his breakfast egg *anywhere.*

He spent most of the day looking, then gave up in disgust and ate cereal instead.

The next day was the same. And the next. And the next. By the end of the week, the farmer had given up looking. Anyway, he was rather enjoying his cereal!

Three weeks later, a cheeping sound came from the henhouse, and all the animals gathered round to see Oona's six beautiful little chicks. Yes, Oona had laid her eggs in the one place the farmer didn't think of looking – back in the henhouse!

The proud mother marched round the farmyard with her brood, and even the farmer couldn't help smiling. He was even more pleased a few months later, when the chicks were grown up and he had more eggs for his breakfast than he could ever eat!

The Cabbage Cruncher

Mr. Jameson's vegetable garden was his pride and joy. He had neat rows of carrots and cabbages, runner beans and radishes, peas and parsnips. There was not a weed, or a slug, or a caterpillar to be seen.

One morning Mr. Jameson had a shock. One of his cabbage leaves had been nibbled! The next morning, a whole cabbage was pretty much munched up.

That evening, Mr. Jameson made himself some sandwiches and a flask of coffee and settled down in his garden shed to keep watch.

Just as the moon was rising, someone came hopping into the garden. A little brown rabbit skipped happily over to the cabbages and started to nibble. A second later, he found himself nose to nose with Mr. Jameson, who had slipped out of the shed in his socks surprisingly quietly.

"What do you think you're doing?" he snarled.

"I'm just a poor, hungry bunny," sobbed the rabbit, "trying to keep going in these hard times. Sob!"

"Good acting," said Mr. Jameson grimly, "but not convincing. You don't look very hungry." Indeed, the cabbage cruncher was pretty plump.

The rabbit looked shrewdly at Mr. Jameson and tried another approach. "I'm so sorry," he said humbly, "but these are just the most beautifully grown, tenderest, juiciest, most delicious cabbages I have ever tasted. I couldn't help myself."

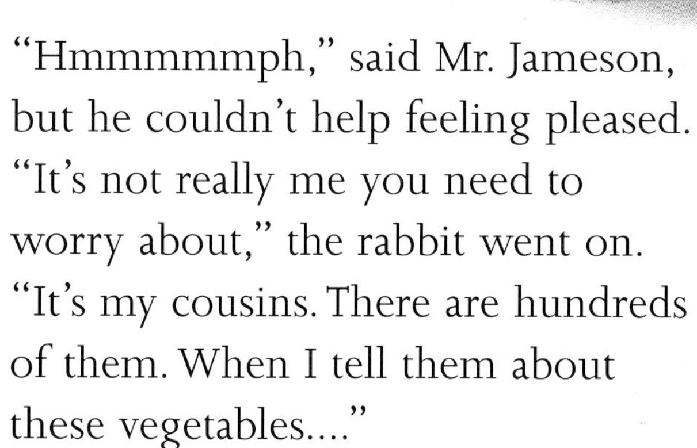

"Hmmmmmph," said Mr. Jameson, but he couldn't help feeling pleased. "It's not really me you need to worry about," the rabbit went on. "It's my cousins. There are hundreds of them. When I tell them about these vegetables...."

Mr. Jameson looked at the rabbit, and the rabbit looked right back.

"If I grew some very, very special cabbages, just for you," said the gardener, "do you think you could keep away from these fairly ordinary ones? And do you think your cousins would need to hear about it?"

"If I was busy dining on your very, very special cabbages, I wouldn't ever have time to see them," smiled the rabbit.

Mr. Jameson and the rabbit live happily side by side these days. And the clever little rabbit is even plumper.

Carenza the Cockatoo

Carenza was a beautiful white cockatoo. She was not a vain bird, but people seemed to like her, so she was proud of her snowy feathers and curly crest. Everything changed when Prudence the parrot began to share her cage.

Prudence was red and blue and green. She looked wonderful. People crowded around the cage to admire her – far more than had admired Carenza.

Carenza began to feel sad. She looked down at her plain feathers and felt, well, under-dressed. Prudence didn't help.

"I do think it's important to have at least a few green feathers," she would say. "They help the red ones look even brighter."

Carenza lost confidence. Her crest flopped, and she lurked at the back of the cage. No one wanted her any more.

Then, one day, the little girl who looked after the birds left the cage door open by mistake. Prudence shuddered and turned away. She was not an adventurous bird. But Carenza had seen something out in the room. Boldly, she stepped outside the cage door and flew over to the table.

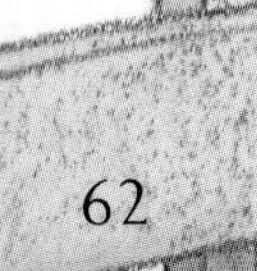

The little girl had left her paints there. Carenza knew just what to do. Within a couple of minutes she had given herself a blue head, a red tummy, one purple wing, one pink wing, a yellow crest and a green back. The colours ran into each other a little bit, but she still thought she looked pretty good.

Just then the little girl returned. Carenza flapped her wings proudly and took up a pose. The little girl didn't smile or clap her hands in admiration. She screamed.

People came running from every direction.

"Oh, my goodness, is it a disease?" cried the little girl's mother. "I've never in my life seen such an awful looking bird."

"But she was so beautiful!" sobbed the little girl.

A visiting uncle, who understood at once what had happened, gently picked Carenza up and took her away to clean her.

Carenza didn't mind a bit. When she returned, her crest was standing up proudly as she joined Prudence in the cage. The admiring look in the little girl's eyes told her everything she needed to know, and she was happy to be herself once more.

Wiggly Worms

Josh loved to help his dad in the garden. Well, Josh called it helping. Sometimes his dad called it other things. Josh was only a little boy, so he couldn't dig or push the wheelbarrow. What he liked to do best of all was to clomp along in his red rubber boots on the soil that his dad had just dug.

One day, as Josh was clomping, he saw something very interesting. It was pink and wriggly. He bent down to pick it up.

"What's this, Dad?" he called.

Dad took one look and shouted,
"It's a worm, Josh. Put it down carefully.
Don't squish it. Don't squash it.
And whatever you do, don't try to eat it!"

Josh didn't want to eat the worm, but he didn't want to put it down, either. He put it in his pocket instead.

That afternoon, Josh had a lovely time. He found eight more worms. Eight times his dad told him to put them down. But he didn't.

At four o'clock, Josh went indoors. He hung up his coat in the hall. He didn't think about the worms, but later, he had spaghetti for his supper, and looking down at his plate reminded him of the squiggly things in his pocket.

"I've just got to go and do something," he told his dad, wriggling down from the table.

"Josh, I told you to go before you sat down," said his mother, but Josh had already left the room.

He hurried to the hall and put his hand into his coat pocket. It was empty. He tried the other pocket. That one was empty, too. Josh looked on the floor, but there was no sign of anything squiggly or wiggly. He went back to his spaghetti with a thoughtful look on his face and somehow didn't feel like eating it after all.

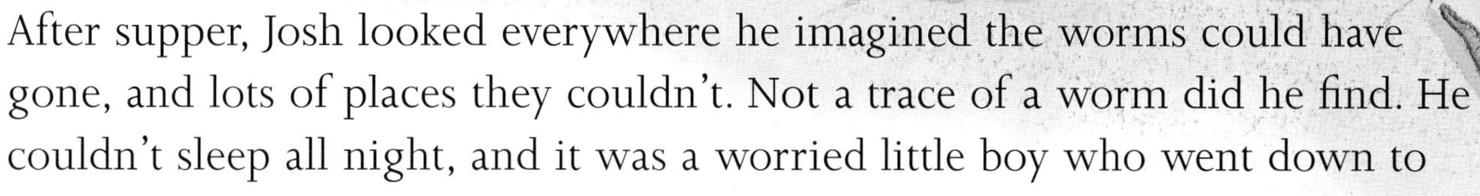

After supper, Josh looked everywhere he imagined the worms could have gone, and lots of places they couldn't. Not a trace of a worm did he find. He couldn't sleep all night, and it was a worried little boy who went down to breakfast that morning. His mother asked him if he was feeling all right.

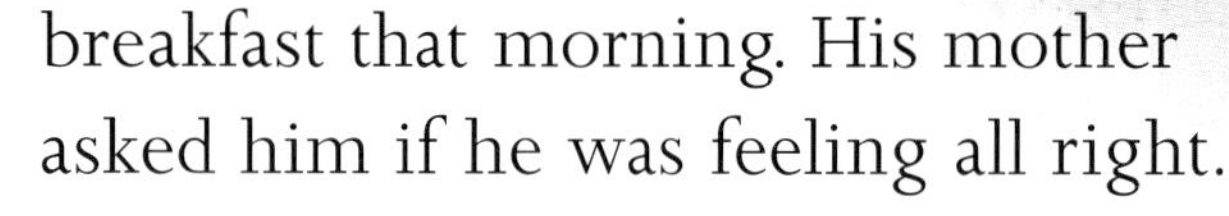

Dad was in a hurry as usual. Waving a piece of toast, he said goodbye to his family and hurried off to put on his coat and catch his train.

Josh was just beginning to think that he was so worried he really *did* feel ill, when there came a terrible yell from the hall.

Josh's mother rushed off to see what had happened, but Josh started spooning in the cereal he had pushed away. He had a big grin on his face and suddenly felt very, very hungry.

A Bird's-eye View

Once upon a time there were three friends who went for a walk in the woods. They were Kitty Cat, Roly Dog and Bobby Rabbit.

"Where are you off to?" asked Biddy Bird. "Can I come?"

"Don't be silly," said Kitty. "We're going for a walk. Birds like you don't walk. You fly. Of course you can't come."

Biddy Bird was upset. "I *can* walk," she said. "Look!"

But Biddy Bird could only hop.
And she couldn't hop quickly like Bobby Rabbit.

"No, no, that's no good," said Roly Dog.
"We're going to walk quickly. See you later!"

So the friends set off. Biddy Bird sat on a branch and felt sad. She hated being left out.

Meanwhile, Kitty and Roly and Bobby walked quickly through the woods. Pretty soon they were very tired.

"I think we should go home now," said Roly. "Come on!"

But which way was home? There were so many paths!

"We're lost," said Bobby.

"Completely lost," agreed Kitty.

"If only we hadn't walked so fast, we might have noticed where we were going," sighed Roly.

Just then, they heard a whistling sound overhead.

"I can help you!" called Biddy Bird.
"From up here I can see where all the paths lead."

So Biddy Bird helped the friends to find their way home. Perhaps *you* can help Biddy.

I don't think Roly and Kitty and Bobby will leave Biddy behind another time, do you?

The Perfect Picnic

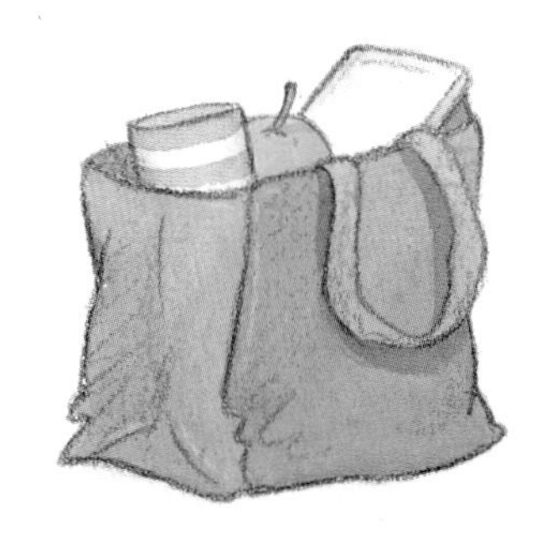

Max Mouse looked out of the window. It was a beautiful sunny day. "Can we have a picnic in the park today, Mamma?" he asked.

"If you leave me in peace this morning and I can get all my work done, we can," said his mother.

So Mamma sat at the table with her papers, and Max sat with her and did some scribbling of his own until...

"Stop!" said Mamma, "you're writing on my work, Max! Now I'll have to do it all again!"

Next, Mamma went into the kitchen and cleared up the breakfast things. Max helped until...

"Stop!" cried Mamma. "You're spilling milk on the floor! Now I'll have to wash that as well!"

When the kitchen was tidy, Mamma went upstairs to collect all the dirty laundry. Max helped to carry it until...

"Stop!" called Mamma. "Those are clean clothes! Now I'll have to sort them all out again."

Max was very hungry by the time Mamma looked at the clock and said, "Oh dear, we'll have to have a late lunch."

"A late picnic," Max reminded her.

"Oh, yes, well, come on, let's get it ready," said his mother.

So they put sandwiches and apples and drinks and yogurts in a bag. Mum answered two phone calls and Max lost one of his trainers, but at last they were ready to go, until…

"Oh no!" said Max. As he opened the front door, there was a loud clap of thunder and rain came pouring down.

Max and Mamma looked at each other. Then Mamma began to laugh. "It's just not our day, Max," she said, "but I've got an idea."

Five minutes later, Max and Mamma were sitting in the middle of the playroom having a wonderful picnic until … the phone began to ring.

"The phone, Mamma!" said Max, when she didn't move.

"I can't hear the phone all the way from the park, can I?" grinned Mamma, staying right where she was. "Let's have another sandwich."

The Sausage Dog

There was once a dog who loved sausages.
He looked a bit like a sausage himself,
and his name was Bruno.

One morning, Bruno was strolling down the street
when he smelled something very interesting. Sausages!
He dashed into Mrs. Potter's house with a glint in his eye. Ten seconds later,
he dashed out again with a string of sausages in his mouth!

"Come back!" yelled Mrs. Potter, dashing out herself.

But Bruno scurried off down the street. Mrs. Potter was quite old. When she got to the end of the street, she was out of breath.

"I'll help you," said Jimmy Jacks, who was on his way to the park. And he rushed off after Bruno and the sausages.

Jimmy was fast, but Bruno had a good start. By the time he and Mrs. Potter reached the next corner, they were both out of breath.

"I'll help," panted Mr. Markham, who was out for his morning jog.

But by the time Mr. Markham and Jimmy Jacks and Mrs. Potter reached the park gates, Bruno and the sausages were even further ahead.

"Woof!" barked a voice nearby. It was Bruce, a dog who liked sausages almost as much as Bruno did. He meant, "I'll help!" in dog language.

So Bruce and Mr. Markham and Jimmy Jacks and Mrs. Potter raced across the park. And although Bruno was fast, his legs were much, much shorter than Bruce's. Bruno reached the edge of the lake with Bruce right behind him.

"Woof! Woof!" barked Bruce, meaning "Drop those sausages!"

"Woof!" barked Bruno, meaning "No way!" But when Bruno opened his mouth to bark, the sausages dropped out, and Bruce quickly grabbed them.

Bruce laid the sausages at panting Mrs. Potter's feet. Mrs. Potter hesitated. Did she really *want* sausages that had been in the mouths of two dogs and dragged halfway across town? She did not. "You can have them, Bruce," she said, "for being such a good dog."

Mrs. Potter, Jimmy Jacks and Mr. Markham walked home. Bruce and Bruno went behind a bush and divided the sausages between them.

"Woof!" said Bruce, with his mouth full.

"Woof! Woof!" agreed Bruno happily. "It works every time!"

Moon Muncher

Oscar was a very small owl. He lived with his parents in a huge oak tree. For the first few weeks of his life all he could think about was food. He opened his little beak and waited for his mother or father to pop something delicious into it. And they did, all night long.

When Oscar got a little bit older, he started to take an interest in other things, too. He found out about his tree and all the other creatures who lived there, although he did not often meet them. Most of them were asleep at night, but Oscar and his family preferred to sleep during the day.

Then, one night, Oscar noticed something else. It was big and round and shiny. It hung among the stars just over the branch where Oscar was sitting.

"It's the moon," explained the little owl's dad. "Isn't it beautiful? We can see it every night if there are no clouds in the way."

The next night, it was a little later when Oscar woke up. He looked above his branch, but there was no moon! "Dad! Dad!" called Oscar.

Dad laughed. "The moon moves across the sky each night," he said. "Look over there!"

It was the moon, looking as beautiful as ever. Oscar was happy.

But over the nights that followed, Oscar became more and more worried. He wasn't sure at first, but at last he knew he was right. Something was eating the moon! It wasn't big and round any more. It was only about half the size it used to be.

Oscar decided that he must find out who was doing this terrible thing. Night after night, he sat on his branch and didn't take his eyes off the slowly moving moon.

"I'm worried about our Oscar," said his mother. "He's hardly eating at all. He just stares at the moon all night."

"I'll have a word with him," promised Dad.

By this time, only a tiny sliver of moon was left. When Dad went to talk to Oscar, he found the little owl crying. "Look at the moon, Dad," sobbed Oscar. "Tomorrow it will all be gone. The moon-muncher has eaten it up."

Dad smiled. "But a new moon will grow, Oscar," he said. "You just wait and see."

Dad was right. Each night, the moon grew a little bit bigger until one night, it was big and round and perfect, and Oscar was happy again.

The Circus Mouse

Titchy Mouse's granny came to stay one winter. She brought Titchy a present. It was a storybook about a circus, and Titchy loved it.

"I'm going to be in a circus one day," he told his little brother Teensy. "I'm going to be a famous tightrope-walker."

Titchy knew that he had some studying to do. He looked out of the window of the old tree stump where his family lived. There was just the thing! His mother had strung her laundry line between two bushes. It was perfect for tightrope-walking.

Getting onto the rope was easy. Titchy climbed up the bush and scampered onto the swaying line. *Ooooo...errrrr!* The line twizzled. Titchy twizzled ... and fell *bump!* on his head.

Teensy laughed so much that tears dripped off his tiny, baby nose.

"Right," said Titchy, brushing himself down. "I might be better at trapeze work." He had often watched the squirrels leaping through the branches of the nearby trees. It didn't look too hard.

Titchy climbed the nearest tree and took a huge leap towards the next branch. He didn't even come close. With a wail he crashed down toward the ground. Luckily, twigs and leaves broke his fall. He landed with a *crunch!*

right next to Teensy, who laughed and laughed until his ears went bright pink.

Titchy sat on the ground and thought. Maybe he really wasn't cut out for an act that took place in the air. What could he do on the ground. "I know!" he cried. "I'll be a lion-tamer!"

In a nearby garden lived an orange cat called Leo. "He'll be fine to practise on until I can find a real lion," said Titchy.

So Titchy armed himself with a chair and set off to find Leo.

It was easy. The cat was asleep in the sun. He didn't like being prodded with a chair, even if it was a tiny one. He gave a yelp and ran off, with Titchy running after him.

"Come back!" yelled Titchy. "I want you to do some tricks!" But Leo just ran faster.

The sight of a mouse chasing a cat sent Teensy into even more giggling and chortling.

"I don't know what's got into you today," said his mother. "You're not usually as cheerful as this, Teensy."

Titchy was catching his breath when he heard this. Suddenly, he knew exactly what he could be. He found a red berry and stuck it on his nose. He found a pair of his dad's shoes and some baggy trousers. He was a clown! And his antics kept Teensy laughing all afternoon.

Titchy had found his dream job at last.

The Magician's Rabbit

Mr. Magic was a magician. He performed at children's parties mainly.

The highlight of Mr. Magic's act was when he pulled a rabbit out of a hat. The audience always clapped and cheered at that point, and that made Mr. Magic happy.

One day, as Mr. Magic got his things ready for a show, the rabbit, who was sitting in the special, comfortable box that Mr. Magic had made for him, suddenly spoke!

"I'm very sorry," said the rabbit with a sigh, "but we won't be able to do the show today. I'm feeling really poorly."

Mr. Magic stood there with his mouth open for a moment. Then he realized what the rabbit had said.

"Do you need a vet?" he asked. "Will you be okay?"

"I'll be fine," said the rabbit. "It's just a cold. But I really couldn't work today. You'll have to tell the children they can't have their show."

"Well," said Mr. Magic, "I'm sorry you're ill, of course. And I want to talk to you later about the fact that you can *speak*. But I'll just do the show by myself and finish with the old patterned handkerchiefs trick instead. It's not as good as you appearing, but it will do."

"You can't do that!" cried the rabbit.

"I can and I will!" replied Mr. Magic. And he shut the rabbit up in his box.

Oh dear. The show was a disaster. The disappearing drink didn't disappear. The magic knots wouldn't come undone. And the patterned handkerchiefs were white. All of them.

At the end of the show, there was no cheering. Mr. Magic was very upset.

"This has never happened before," he muttered, as he loaded his boxes back into his car.

"I told you," said a muffled voice.

It was the rabbit. Mr. Magic opened the box. "I told you not to do the show," said the rabbit, "but you wouldn't listen."

"You mean I was so upset that you were ill that I couldn't do anything right?" asked Mr. Magic.

"No, you noodle!" shouted the rabbit. "It isn't you who does the magic. It's me! Usually. *I'm* the magician."

Mr. Magic was stunned. "Prove it," he said.

"Remember I'm not well," groaned the rabbit. But still, he produced a cup of coffee out of thin air. Mr. Magic drank the coffee – he felt he needed it – and thought about what the rabbit had said. At last he spoke.

"I will rename my act "Mr. Magic and Co." he said. "No one will guess that you are really Mr. Magic and I am 'and Co.' Oh, and one more thing...."

"I know," said the new Mr. Magic. And he magicked the coffee cup away.

The Lady and the Bird

Many years ago, a very rich lady kept a beautiful bird in a cage. The bird was not very big, but she was gorgeous. She had red and pink and orange feathers. She hated living in a cage.

One day, the bird decided that enough was enough. "I want to go out and about," she told the rich lady. "I want to be out in the open air. I want to see everything and go everywhere."

"But if I let you out of your cage, you'll fly away," said the lady.

"No, I won't," said the bird. But, of course, as soon as the lady opened the door, she was off. She flew out through the open window and into the street.

It was wonderful being outside, but the bird knew nothing of city ways. She had grown up in a rainforest far away. She flew straight into a telephone wire and hurt her wing.

The poor bird fluttered down onto a windowsill to rest. Almost at once, a huge cat pounced on her and hurt her other wing. The poor bird could hardly fly at all now. She hopped and fluttered from windowsill to windowsill. By evening, she was very hungry and very tired.

By luck, the bird had fluttered last of all onto her very own windowsill! She didn't realize it, but the lady, sitting sadly inside, spotted her and cried out with delight. She picked the bird up carefully and carried her to the cage.

But the little bird shuddered and hid her head under her wing. Even though she was tired and hurt and hungry, she liked being free.

The lady was not unkind, and she noticed. She put the bird down on a chair and went to get her some food and water.

When she came back, the lady was smiling and dressed to go out. As the little bird ate and drank, she explained her plan.

"I know you want to see the wide world," she said, "and so do I. Why don't we do it together? Hop onto my hat, and we can travel wherever we like."

The little bird looked up. The lady was wearing a beautiful red and pink and orange hat. In the middle there was a place where a red and pink and orange bird could sit very comfortably and never be noticed at all.

So that is what they did. If you ever see a lady in a large red and pink and orange hat, look carefully. She may not be alone!

Index of Themes